Linc

D0474462

The Furry Detectives

Diana Kimpton

Illustrated by
Desideria Gucciardini

The Clamerkin Clan

Hilton

Amy

Einstein

Plato

Isambard

Bun

Willow

To Anton

First published in the UK in 2010 by Usborne Publishing Ltd., Usborne House, 83-85 Saffron Hill, London EC1N 8RT, England. www.usborne.com

Text copyright © Diana Kimpton, 2010

Illustration copyright © Usborne Publishing Ltd., 2010

The name Usborne and the devices ♆ ⊕ are Trade Marks of Usborne Publishing Ltd.

Cover photograph © Getty Images/Tim Platt

A CIP catalogue record for this book is available from the British Library.

 FMAMJJASOND/10 95175   ISBN 9781409504320

Printed in Reading, Berkshire. UK.

CHAPTER ONE

"What are you doing?" asked Amy Wild, as she stepped into the kitchen.

Mum peered out from under the table. "I'm looking for my ring. I took it off last night when I was washing up and forgot to put it on again. Now there's no sign of it anywhere."

"I can't find it either," barked Hilton, the cairn terrier. But Mum didn't realize he was speaking. Only Amy understood what he said.

She bent down and tickled the dog's ears. Then she looked at Mum and asked, "Can you remember where you put it?"

"I'm sure it was on the window sill," Mum replied. She crawled out from under the table and stood up. "I've already looked there, but it would be great if you did too. Your eyes are sharper than mine."

Amy leaned over the sink and searched among the potted plants lined up in front of the open window. Mum was right. The ring wasn't there. "Maybe Dad or Granty moved it," Amy suggested.

"No, I asked them." Mum slumped down in a chair, and put her head in her hands. "I wouldn't mind so much if it was any other bit of jewellery. But Dad gave me that ring when he asked me to marry him."

"I'm sorry," said Amy. "It must be awful losing something that special." She would be heartbroken if she lost the string of glittering paws that hung around her neck. Without its secret power, she wouldn't be able to talk to animals any more. And she couldn't be a member of the clan – the

group of animals that looked after Clamerkin Island.

"It looks as if it's gone for good," said Mum with a sigh.

Suddenly, Amy noticed the curtains blowing in the breeze. "Don't give up yet," she said, as she pointed them out to Mum. "Maybe they knocked the ring into the sink."

Her suggestion threw Mum into a panic. "It's gone down the plughole! I'm sure it has. Quick! Run and get Dad. He might be able to get it out of the drain before it's washed away."

Amy raced out of the kitchen, pushed open the swing door at the end of the hall and stepped into the public part of her home. The Primrose Tea

Room was busy. There were customers
sitting at all the tables, and the air
was filled with chattering voices and
the clinking of cups.

Amy found Dad behind the counter
with her great-aunt, Granty. "Mum
needs you in the kitchen straight
away," she said, as she tugged urgently
on his sleeve. "She thinks her ring's
gone down the plughole."

"Oh dear," said Dad, and he strode
away through the swing door.

Amy started to follow him. But a
border collie bounded out from under
a nearby table and blocked her path.

"Don't go," he barked. "I need the
clan's help."

Amy bent down and stroked him.

10

She put her head close to his so no one else could hear what she was saying. Then she asked, "What's wrong?"

Before the dog had a chance to reply, an old lady rushed up and clipped a lead onto his collar. "You're a naughty dog, Barney," she scolded. Then she

turned to Amy and said, "I'm so sorry. He doesn't usually misbehave."

"That's all right, Mrs. Winthrop," said Amy. The dog's owner was one of the Primroses's regular customers and she was usually full of smiles. But today she looked unhappy. Was that just because of Barney's bad behaviour or was something else wrong?

"Please call me Flora, my dear," replied the old lady. "Everyone else does, and Barney certainly seems to like you."

The dog gazed trustingly at Amy. "We've got to talk," he whimpered.

Amy knew that. But she also knew that it would be hard to talk in the tea room without attracting attention.

Granty was the only other person in the world who knew Amy could talk to animals – she didn't want anyone else asking what she was doing. "Perhaps Barney's bored," she suggested. "Would you like me to take him out in the garden?"

"I'm sure he'd love that," said Flora, as she handed Amy the lead. "But don't be long. We're going home as soon as I've finished my tea and cake."

Amy gave the lead a slight tug and called, "Come on, Barney." The dog didn't need any more encouragement. He trotted eagerly beside her through the swing door and down the hall.

They had almost reached the back door when Hilton ran out of the kitchen.

"What's Barney doing here?" he asked.

"Asking the clan for help," said Amy.

"Great," barked Hilton, wagging his tail. "Shall I call the others?"

"There isn't time. He's got to go soon." She opened the back door and led the collie outside.

But Barney stopped on the doorstep and sniffed the air. He gave a low growl as the hackles on his neck rose. Then he bounded forward, barking, "Cat! Cat! Cat!"

The sudden movement almost pulled Amy off her feet. "Stop!" she yelled, as she tugged hard on the lead.

But Barney took no notice. All his attention was on the Siamese cat curled up in the sunshine in the middle of the

lawn. "Cat! Cat!" he barked, as he ran towards it.

The cat jumped up in alarm and raced off across the grass. Barney hurtled after the streak of cream fur, towing Amy behind him. Her arm felt as if it was being pulled out of its socket but she didn't dare let go of the lead. Barney was in her care – what would she say to Flora if she lost him?

CHAPTER TWO

The cat shot under some bushes,
obviously hoping to shake off her pursuer.
But it would take more than that to stop
Barney. He dived after her, leaving Amy
with no choice but to follow.

Barney was small enough to run under
the branches, but Amy wasn't. Twigs
tugged and scratched her as the dog
pulled her through the bushes. She put

her spare arm across her face and closed her eyes to protect them.

Suddenly, the pull on her other arm disappeared. Amy felt a wave of panic. Had the lead broken? Had she lost Flora's dog? Then she opened her eyes and saw that Barney was still there. He had stopped pulling because he had stopped running.

The dog was standing at the bottom of an old apple tree, staring up into its branches. Then he jumped up on his hind legs with his front paws on the trunk and barked, "Cat! Cat! Cat!"

A loud hissing came from above his head. Amy looked up and saw the Siamese cat balanced on a branch.

Her back was arched, and her tail stood straight up like a bottlebrush. Amy waved at her and asked, "Are you all right, Willow?"

"I suppose so," grumbled the cat. "But that's no thanks to your friend there."

Amy stared disapprovingly at Barney. "I thought you wanted the clan to help you?"

"I do," he said. "But there was this cat and I always chase cats. It's what dogs do."

"No, it's not," barked Hilton, who had arrived in time to hear the conversation. "Especially if the cat concerned is a member of the clan."

Barney's eyes opened wide in

astonishment. "Has the clan got a cat in it?"

"Four, to be exact," said Willow from her branch. She stuck her nose in the air in a superior way and added, "In fact, we're in the majority. There's only one human."

"That's Amy," said Hilton.

Willow scowled at him and continued. "There's only one dog."

"That's me," barked Hilton, bouncing up and down with excitement.

Willow scowled at him again. "I suppose you're going to tell him all about the only parrot."

"That's Plato," said Hilton. "But he doesn't come out much. He likes to stay in the living room watching TV."

Barney's ears and tail drooped. "I'm sorry," he said in a very subdued voice. "I didn't realize I was chasing someone so important. Will you still help me?"

"Of course we will," said Amy, as she sat down next to him and stroked his head. "Won't we, Willow?"

"I suppose so," said the Siamese cat. She stretched out her front legs and started  to sharpen her claws on the branch. "What's the problem?"

"There are two actually and they are both making my human miserable."

Amy nodded. "I'd noticed she looks sad. That's not like her at all. Last time I spoke to her she was really excited about going to her grandson's wedding."

"That's one of the problems," Barney sighed. "It's tomorrow morning and she's been looking forward to it for months. She's even bought a new dress for herself and a matching bow for me."

Hilton collapsed in giggles. "You! With a bow!"

Amy nudged him with her elbow. "Don't laugh. It's rude," she whispered. Then she stroked Barney's head again and said, "I'm sure you'll look lovely."

"I probably won't," said the dog with another huge sigh. "But it doesn't matter anyway. Flora's friend has got the flu so she can't look after the sheep and chickens while we are away. And that means we can't go."

"Can't your human ask someone else?" asked Willow, as she climbed down from the tree.

"She has," said Barney. "But everyone's too busy, and we're running out of time. If we don't catch the last boat today, we'll be too late for the wedding."

"No wonder she's sad," said Amy.

Barney gazed at them with big, trusting eyes and wagged his tail. "That's why I've come to you. You're the clan. You must be able to do something."

Amy bit her lip thoughtfully. "Are sheep and chickens hard to look after?"

"Easy-peasy," said Hilton. "Sheep are stupid. They just stand in a field and eat grass."

"And the chickens just need feeding and shutting up at night to keep them safe from foxes," added Barney.

"I'm sure I could do that," said Amy. "There's no more school until Monday so I've plenty of time. And it would be fun to collect the eggs."

"I suppose it might be," said Barney in a voice tinged with doubt, "if it wasn't for the other problem."

"Which is?" asked Hilton.

"The disappearing eggs. My human thinks the chickens have stopped laying. But the chickens say they haven't. They say they lay the eggs as normal, but they vanish."

Hilton made a choking sound as he tried not to giggle again. "Eggs can't vanish."

"That's what I used to think," said Barney. "But I was wrong."

Before Amy had a chance to ask any more questions, Granty called her from the Primrose. "Bring Barney back now, Amy. Flora's ready to leave."

Amy jumped to her feet. "Come on," she said. "Let's tell Flora that I'll look after her animals."

"At least that will solve one problem," said Willow.

As Amy led the collie down the hall,

she stopped by the kitchen door and
saw Mum and Dad in front of the sink.
"Any luck?" she asked.

"Yes and no," said Dad with a smile. "The good news is that the ring can't have gone down the plughole. It's too big to fit through."

"The bad news is that we still can't find it," added Mum.

Dad scratched his head thoughtfully. "We've looked everywhere. I can't think what's happened to it."

"It's a real mystery," said Mum, with a sigh. "The ring's completely disappeared."

Just like the eggs, thought Amy. Surely that was just coincidence. The two mysteries couldn't possibly be connected...could they?

CHAPTER THREE

When Amy and Barney reached the
tea room, they found Flora by the
counter talking to Granty. The old
lady still looked sad, but she smiled
weakly when Barney licked her hand.

Amy knew she must be careful. She
couldn't admit she had talked to
Barney without giving away the secret
of the necklace. So she had to find some

other way to volunteer to help. "Are you ready for your grandson's wedding?" she asked.

Flora's smile vanished as quickly as it had arrived. "I can't go." She sighed. "There's no one to look after my animals."

"That's dreadful," said Granty. "Surely there's someone who can help. I'd do it myself if only I had the time.'"

"That's the problem," said Flora, as she wiped away a tear. "Everyone I've asked is too busy."

"What about me?" said Amy. "I'm sure I can look after sheep and chickens." She realized too late that Flora hadn't mentioned which animals she had. Luckily the old lady didn't

notice her mistake. But Granty did. She
winked at Amy and nodded towards
Barney to show she'd guessed where the
extra information had come from.

"I'm not sure," said Flora. "Aren't you
busy with school?"

"It's the weekend," said Amy. "And I
haven't any homework."

Flora still looked doubtful, "It's asking an awful lot of someone so young."

"Amy's brilliant with animals," said Granty. "I'm sure she could manage."

"I'm sure I could too," said Amy. "And I can go back with you now so you can show me what to do."

Flora hesitated. Then she smiled broadly and said, "That would be lovely."

To Amy's surprise, Flora called a taxi to take them back to her cottage. "We need to hurry," she explained. "I've got to show you what to do, collect my things and get down to the harbour in time to catch the last ferry."

"I love taxis," said Barney, as he

jumped into the back seat and stretched out. Amy and Hilton squeezed into the small amount of space left while Flora sat in the front. It didn't take long to reach her home. The cottage stood on the edge of town, near the top of the hill, and it had beautiful views of the sea that surrounded the Island.

Flora didn't stop to look at the view. As soon as Amy and Hilton were out of the taxi, she led the way to a field behind the cottage. "These are my sheep," she announced, waving her arm towards the five mounds of wool, busily munching the grass. The sheep looked up at the sound of her voice and trotted over to the gate.

Flora introduced them each in turn. "This is Floss, Drum, Sprig, Clover and Tallulah. I bottle-fed them all when they were lambs, and I couldn't bear to part with them when they grew up."

"Do I have to feed them?" asked Amy, as she patted their woolly heads.

"No, they've got plenty of grass. You just need to check that they haven't escaped and that they are all the right way up."

Amy's eyes widened in surprise. Hilton was more dramatic. He rolled on his back, laughing. "I told you sheep are stupid," he barked. "They can't even stay upright without help."

All five sheep looked offended. "There's no need to be rude," Sprig bleated.

"It's not our fault," grumbled Floss. "It's all this wool."

"It makes rolling over very difficult," said Drum.

"Sometimes we get stuck on our backs," added Tallulah.

The explanation made sense to Amy.

But it didn't calm Hilton down. He continued to roar with laughter.

Flora watched his behaviour in dismay. To her, the laughter sounded like barking. "I hope your dog's not going to chase my sheep."

Her words brought Hilton to his senses. His tail stopped wagging and his ears drooped. "Sorry," he whimpered. "I didn't mean to worry anyone. I'll wait in the taxi with Barney so I don't cause any more problems."

"I'll make sure he behaves," Amy promised, as she watched him walk away. "Now what do I have to do with the chickens?"

"The really important thing is to shut them safely in the henhouse before the sun goes down. I don't want a fox to catch them." Flora went into the shed, fetched a scoop full of chicken food and handed it to Amy. "They need feeding inside their house in the evening and outside in the morning. You try, my dear. It's time they came in and it will be good practice for you. They always

come easily when they see their dinner."

Amy rattled the food in the scoop and called, "Chickens. Come along, chickens."

There was a rustling in the bushes. Then three golden brown hens scuttled into view. "They're called Faith, Hope and Charity," said Flora, pointing to each one in turn.

"Oooh, someone new," said Faith, as she peered at Amy.

"She looks like the Talker," clucked Hope. "The one the sparrows have been telling us about."

"Stop dithering," said Charity, as she headed for the henhouse. "The sooner we're inside, the sooner we can eat."

Amy followed the chickens into their home, tipped the food into their bowl and checked they had enough water. Then she stepped outside and fastened the door carefully.

This seemed a good moment to bring up the subject of the disappearing eggs. But she had to be careful – she mustn't admit that Barney had told her about them. So she pretended that she knew nothing about the problem and asked, "Where shall I put the eggs in the morning?"

Flora sighed. "I don't expect you'll find any. My hens haven't laid any eggs for three whole weeks."

Her claim was met by squawks of protest from inside the henhouse. All the chickens were talking at once and their voices were muffled by the wooden wall. But Amy was sure she heard someone say "Stolen" and someone else say "Thief".

At that moment, the taxi driver hooted for them to hurry up. "If we don't leave soon, you'll miss the last boat," he called.

"I must get my things," said Flora

and she rushed back to the cottage. Amy went with her to help and saw a suitcase lying open on the bed. Luckily, it was nearly full. The old lady had done most of her packing before her friend had told her she couldn't look after the animals.

"Pass me my butterfly brooch from the dressing table," said Flora, as she tossed her washbag and towel into the case.

Amy found the dressing table easily. It was in front of the window, and its top was neat and tidy. There was a photo of Barney with one of the sheep, a jar of face cream and a box decorated with a shell from the beach. But there was no sign of a brooch.

Amy searched the surrounding floor
and peered underneath the dressing
table and the bed. But the brooch
wasn't there. "I can't see it anywhere,"
she said.

"That's strange," said Flora, as she reached past Barney's photo and shut the window. "I remember putting it here ready to pack, and I remember seeing it just before I went out. But now it's vanished."

Just like the eggs, thought Amy. *And Mum's ring.* Suddenly she remembered that the ring had been beside an open window too. Maybe that was just another coincidence, but maybe it wasn't. Could the chickens be right? Was there a thief at work on Clamerkin Island?

CHAPTER FOUR

Amy decided not to mention her suspicions to Flora. She had no proof that anything had been stolen, and she didn't want to worry the old lady unnecessarily.

Flora flung her hairbrush into the case and shut the lid. "I'll have to go without the brooch," she declared, as she fastened the catches. "There isn't time to find it now."

The taxi driver was worried about the time too. He put the case in the boot, while Flora locked the cottage and climbed into the taxi with Amy and the waiting dogs. Then he drove off at top speed, determined to get the old lady to the harbour before the last boat left.

They nearly didn't make it. The crew were just starting to take up the gangway when the taxi screeched to a halt beside them.

Amy threw open the back door and jumped out. "Don't go yet," she begged. "You've got another passenger."

To her relief, the crew agreed to wait.

They made sure Flora, Barney and the suitcase were safely on board before they finally set sail. The old lady smiled broadly as she waved goodbye from the ship's rail.

"It's good to see her looking so much happier," said Amy, as she waved back.

Hilton barked his agreement. "That problem was easy to solve."

"But the other one is more complicated than we thought," said Amy. "The eggs aren't the only things that are disappearing."

Hilton pricked up his ears. "Tell me more."

"Not yet," replied Amy. "Let's call a clan meeting so I can tell everyone my suspicions at once."

Hilton ran on ahead to call the others together, while Amy walked back to the Primrose on her own. She popped into the kitchen to say she was back. Then she headed for the garden.

The clan's almost-secret meeting place was at the far end, in the middle of a large clump of bushes. She pushed her way through the branches into the clearing in the middle and discovered she was the last to arrive. Hilton was already there and so were the four cats. To her surprise, Plato had come too.

"Hilton made this sound most mysterious," explained the parrot. "Much better than watching repeats on TV."

"I hope it won't take long," said a fat black cat called Bun. "It's almost time for my supper and I'm hungry."

"You're always hungry," grumbled Isambard. He lived with the local mechanic and his tabby coat was smeared with oil stains.

Willow, the Siamese from the post office, stood up and stuck her tail in the air. "Stop complaining, both of you. I want to hear Amy's news."

Amy waited until they'd settled down. Then she told them about the lost ring, the missing brooch and the disappearing eggs. "We won't know for sure until we speak to the chickens. But from what I heard, it sounds as if there might be a thief at work."

Bun shuddered. "Scary things, thieves. Perhaps you should tell the police."

"Not yet," said Amy. "We've no proof that anything's been stolen.

We need to find out more before we bother anyone else."

"We can be detectives," squawked Plato, jumping up and down in excitement. "Can I be Inspector Lake? I love watching him on TV."

"I'd rather be Sherlock Holmes," said Einstein, the white Persian cat from the school. "The senior class were learning about him the other day."

Hilton wagged his tail. "This is going to be fun. Let's get started."

"We can't," said Amy. "The first thing we've got to do is talk to the chickens. But they've already gone to bed so we can't do that until tomorrow."

*

The clan had arranged to meet the next morning at Flora's cottage. Amy, Hilton and Plato were the first to arrive. "I can see some thieves already," barked the cairn terrier, as he scampered after the pigeons raiding the cabbage patch.

The pigeons flew into the air in a cloud of grey wings and settled in a nearby tree. Their arrival disturbed the birds that were already there. One with a green head flew off to another tree, a pair of blue tits went to investigate Flora's flowers and a big black and white bird glided down to join the sheep in their field. They took no notice of the new

arrival. They just went on grazing.

Amy was pleased to see that all five sheep were there and all five sheep were the right way up. She didn't need to do anything else with them today so she could concentrate on the investigation.

She fetched some chicken food from the shed and walked over to the henhouse with Hilton and Plato. Just as she reached it, the four cats from the clan came running up.

"Sorry we're late," said Willow.

"It's Bun's fault," grumbled Isambard.

"He wouldn't leave until he'd eaten his breakfast," explained Einstein.

Bun licked his lips and purred. "It's easier to be a detective on a full stomach."

The chickens rushed out of the henhouse as soon as Amy opened the door. Faith and Hope immediately spotted the assembled clan and nodded

their heads in greeting. But Charity
only had eyes for the bowl in Amy's
hand. "Breakfast!" she clucked, as she
hopped up and down.

Amy sprinkled the food on the
ground as Flora had instructed. Then
she slipped into the henhouse while the

chickens were pecking it up. She peered into each of the nesting boxes, but they were all empty. There were no eggs lying on the straw.

"Flora was right," she said, as she stepped outside. "You have all stopped laying."

"That's not true," wailed Faith. "I laid an egg this morning, just before dawn."

"But it's gone," said Hope. "It's been stolen, just like all the others."

"So it's true," squawked Plato. "There really is a thief."

"Is he big?" asked Bun in a squeaky voice. He glanced nervously over his shoulder as if he expected someone to jump out of the bushes behind him.

"He can't be," clucked Faith. "He manages to get into the henhouse without opening the door and without us seeing him."

"No one big could do that," said Hope.

Charity stopped eating for a moment and gazed at Amy. "We'd be sure to notice a human, even a young one like you."

"So the thief must be an animal," said Amy. "A small animal." She was glad she hadn't bothered the police. An animal thief was definitely a job for the clan. But how were they going to find out who it was?

CHAPTER FIVE

The clan sat in a circle wondering what to do next. "Inspector Lake would interview all the suspects," said Plato.

"We haven't got any," said Isambard.

"Sherlock Holmes would examine the ground for footprints," said Einstein.

"There aren't any," said Isambard. "The ground's too hard."

Willow stuck her tail in the air and scowled. "You're good at rubbishing other people's ideas," she grumbled. "Have you got any of your own?"

The tabby cat licked his grubby paw thoughtfully. "We're animal detectives. We should be using animal skills."

"Like my nose," said Hilton. He jumped to his feet and rushed right around the henhouse, sniffing the ground carefully.

"Can you smell anything?" asked Amy when he got back.

"Lots," said Hilton, with a doggy grin. "You, me, pigeons, grass, chickens—"

"What about the thief?" Plato interrupted. "Can you smell him?"

The dog put his nose to the ground again and took a huge sniff. "There is one smell that's quite different from all the others."

"A clue! A clue!" squawked Plato, jumping up and down with excitement. "I bet that smell belongs to the thief."

"What sort of animal is it?" asked Amy.

Hilton put his head on one side and half closed his eyes as he thought hard. "I don't know," he admitted eventually. "I'm sure I've smelled something like it before, but I can't remember what it is."

"Sherlock Holmes always understands clues," said Einstein.

"Sherlock Holmes isn't here," snapped Willow.

Hope pecked politely at Amy's trainers to attract her attention. "Have we solved the mystery yet? Only I feel an egg coming on and I want to know if it's safe to lay it."

Her words gave Amy an idea. "Let's

set a trap," she suggested. "Then we can catch the thief red-handed."

"Red-pawed," corrected Plato.

"Or red-clawed," said Willow.

"Do you mean a mousetrap?" asked Bun.

"No. This is a thief trap," Amy explained. "We'll all hide while Hope lays her egg. Then we'll wait until the thief arrives."

"And then we jump on him," shouted Isambard.

Einstein looked worried. "I don't want any violence. I'm going home if there's going to be violence."

"Don't worry," said Amy. "No one is going to get hurt. Not even the thief."

"But we've got to stop him," said Hilton.

"Of course we have," agreed Amy. "But not until he's gone into the henhouse and stolen the egg. He's got to do that before we can be sure he really is the thief."

The clan members spread out around the henhouse and hid themselves carefully in the undergrowth. Amy found that difficult to do because she was so much bigger than the others. But eventually she found a good spot underneath a bush with low hanging branches. Then she waved at Hope to tell her to get started.

The chicken attacked her part with enthusiasm. She strode into the henhouse and started to squawk loudly. Then she strutted out with her head held high.  "I've laid an egg," she announced proudly. "It's a beautiful egg. A big egg. The best egg I've ever laid." She looked around carefully. Then she added at the top of her voice, "I hope no one is going to steal it."

For a moment, nothing happened. Amy wondered if her idea was going to fail. Perhaps the thief was too far away to hear Hope. Perhaps he had stolen enough eggs now and didn't need another one.

Suddenly there was a slight rustling in the grass. Amy looked towards the source of the sound and spotted a small, brown animal heading towards the chickens. He had a long body, and his legs were so short that his belly was low to the ground.

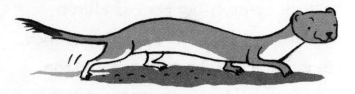

Amy stayed completely still as she watched him. So did the other members of the clan. No one wanted to frighten the new arrival away before they found out if he was the thief.

It was soon obvious that he was. When he reached the henhouse, he glanced furtively over his shoulder without spotting that he was being watched. Then he wriggled through a small hole in the wall and vanished inside. The clan instantly edged forward, ready to surround him when he made his getaway.

"It's a weasel," whispered Hilton, as he wriggled forward on his stomach. He wrinkled his nose and sniffed the air. "That's definitely the smell I picked up before."

The robbery didn't take long. After only a couple of minutes, the weasel reappeared rolling Hope's egg in front of him. He looked very pleased with himself and was so confident that he didn't bother to check if the coast was clear.

It wasn't. Amy waited until he was about a metre away from the henhouse. Then she called, "Now!" and the clan closed in around the weasel. Amy and Hilton blocked the path in front of him while the cats blocked his escape from the sides and rear. The weasel couldn't even jump to safety. Plato made sure of that by flying low over his head.

The weasel stopped and looked around at his captors. Then he sat up on his hind legs and asked innocently, "Is there something wrong?"

"Of course there is," said Willow.

"I'm sorry to hear that," said the weasel. "Now I'd appreciate it if you all moved so I can get on my way with my egg."

"But that's what's wrong," said Einstein. "It's not your egg. It's Hope's."

"It *was* her egg, you mean. Now it's mine. Finders keepers." The weasel dropped back on all fours and tried to roll the egg between Amy and Hilton.

Amy moved sideways to block his path, while Hilton gave a low, warning growl.

The weasel stopped again and scowled at them. "There's no need to be unfriendly."

Amy wagged a finger at him. "You should be ashamed of yourself. Didn't

your mother teach you it was wrong
to steal?"

"No," said the weasel. "She taught me
how to do it." He gave a proud smile
and added, "My dear old mum said I
was the best thief in the whole litter."

Isambard glared at him. "You can't
be that good or we wouldn't have
caught you."

The weasel shifted uneasily from foot
to foot. "You've got a point, I suppose.
What are you going to do now?"

"I'm going to take this away for a
start," said Amy, as she grabbed the
egg. "Then I want you to give back the
ring and the brooch."

"What are you talking about?" asked
the weasel.

"I'm talking about Mum's ring – the one you took from our kitchen. And Flora's brooch – the one you took from her bedroom."

The weasel shook his head. "That's not me. No self-respecting weasel raids human houses. They're far too dangerous. And what would I do with a ring and a brooch anyway? There's no point in stealing something I can't eat."

"He sounds as if he's telling the truth," squawked Plato.

"Of course I am," said the weasel. "I might be a thief, but I'm not a liar."

Amy stared at him in confusion. If he hadn't taken the jewellery, what had happened to it? Had it just got mislaid or was there a second thief on the Island?

CHAPTER SIX

"Can I have my egg back now?" asked the weasel.

"No," said Amy.

He smiled at her and twitched his whiskers. "Can I have it if I tell you who took the ring?"

"That would be telling tales," said Bun.

"Exactly," said the weasel. "And I

think that tale is worth an egg."

"I'm surprised at you," said Plato. "I thought there was honour amongst thieves."

The weasel laughed. "Not in my family there's not. As my dear old

mum always said, 'Do whatever it takes to get out of trouble.'"

Amy rolled the egg in her hands as she wondered what to do. It was smooth and brown and still slightly warm from when it was laid. Flora would be so pleased to see it when she got back.

"I don't mind if you give it to him,"

said Hope. "I wasn't planning to keep it anyway."

Amy still wasn't sure. It felt wrong to let the weasel have the thing he had stolen. That was almost like saying that stealing was all right. But she really *did* want to know what had happened to Mum's ring. If only there was another way.

Then she had an idea. She looked thoughtfully at the weasel. "You said you wouldn't take the ring because you couldn't eat it."

"That's right. Us weasels think our stomachs are important."

"So do some cats," said Willow, looking pointedly at Bun.

Amy ignored the Siamese cat's

interruption and continued. "So the other thief can't be a weasel. It must be some other sort of animal."

"One that likes things it can't eat," said Isambard.

"One that likes things that look pretty," said Hilton.

Einstein gave a purr of satisfaction. "This is deduction, this is. This is what Sherlock Holmes would do."

"It's a bit like a TV quiz," squawked Plato. He put on a silly quizmaster's voice and asked, "Which animal likes stealing glittery, shiny things?"

The rest of the clan looked at him expectantly. "You're the one who spends hours watching quiz shows," said Hilton. "Do you know the answer?"

"Nearly. It's on the tip of my tongue." The parrot scratched his head  thoughtfully and added, "It's some sort of bird, but I can't remember the name. It's big. It's black and white."

Suddenly Amy remembered the birds the pigeons had disturbed when they flew into the tree. "I saw a bird like that this morning..."

"Magpie!" Plato squawked triumphantly. "That's the name I was looking for. It's a magpie."

"That's not fair," said the weasel. "Now you've guessed, I've got nothing to bargain with."

"That's right," said Hilton.

"So it's time I was going." The weasel dived sideways and shot between Bun's legs. He'd chosen his direction well. The black cat was too fat and slow to stop him.

Amy, Hilton and the other cats jumped after the weasel. But there wasn't space for all of them on such a small patch of ground. Amy tripped over Willow and collided with Einstein, while Hilton cannoned into Isambard.

As they crashed down in a heap, the egg slipped out of Amy's grasp. She tried to catch it, but she was too late. It hit the ground and smashed to pieces.

"Bother," said Amy.

"Yummy," said Bun, as he licked up the yolk.

Plato looked at Amy and asked, "What about the weasel?"

"We can deal with him later," she replied. "Right now we've got a magpie to sort out."

Amy led the way to the sheep's field and was pleased to see that the black and white bird was still there. The magpie was striding around between the sheep. Every now and then, she stopped and pecked at something on the ground. Then she strode off again, looking intently at the grass. She was so busy that she didn't notice the clan was watching.

Amy decided it was better if things stayed like that for the time being. She beckoned to the others and led them back to the henhouse to think of a plan.

"Are we going to lay a trap like we did with the weasel?" asked Willow.

"I only do eggs," clucked Hope. "I can't lay a ring."

Bun stared at the string of paws around Amy's neck. "We could use the necklace as bait. It's very shiny."

"Not when Amy's not wearing it," said Hilton. "It turns dull brown when she takes it off."

"That's a stupid idea anyway," added Isambard. "We need Amy to talk to us, and she can't do that without the necklace."

"No trap then," said Amy. "We need some other way to prove that the magpie stole Mum's ring." She looked at Einstein and asked, "What would Sherlock Holmes do now?"

The white Persian cat shook his fluffy head. "I'm not sure. Maybe he would… um…er—"

Plato interrupted him with a loud squawk. "Inspector Lake would search the suspect's house."

Amy grinned. "That's a great idea." She pointed at a tangled mass of twigs in the tree where she had first seen the magpie. "That must be her nest up there."

"It's very high," said Bun. "I don't think I could climb that far."

"Neither could I," said Einstein.

Amy laughed. "You don't have to. We've got Plato. He can fly up to it to see what's inside." She was sure the parrot would be delighted to do some real detective work. But, to her dismay, he wasn't.

He shook his head and looked very serious. "I can't do that. Not without a search warrant."

CHAPTER SEVEN

"What is a search warrant?" asked
Isambard.

"Can you eat it?" asked Bun
hopefully.

"Of course you can't," said Plato. He
fluffed out his chest feathers proudly
and explained, "A search warrant is a
very important piece of paper with
writing on it. Inspector Lake would

never search anywhere without one."

"Perhaps you could get one in the post office," Willow suggested. "My human often gives people important bits of paper."

"That's too far to go," said Hilton. "The magpie might have gone by the time we get back."

Amy wasn't sure the post office was the solution anyway. They weren't *real* detectives so they wouldn't be able to get a *real* search warrant. But she didn't want to upset Plato by telling him so.

She searched through her pockets and found an empty paper bag in one of them. In the other, she found a stub of blue crayon. She laid the bag on the ground and smoothed it out as carefully as she could. Then she picked up the crayon and started to write.

SEARCH WARRANT

This important piece of paper gives Plato permission to search the magpie's nest!

When she had finished, she held up the paper for everyone to see and then she read out the words.

"Perfect," said Plato. "I'm sure Inspector Lake would approve of that." He waited while Amy folded the paper bag. Then he took it proudly in his beak and flew up into the branches.

The clan sat at the bottom of the tree, looking up and waiting. They watched Plato land. They heard him say "Oooh!" and "Aaah!" and "That's pretty." Then they saw him fly down again with something in his beak that glinted in the sunshine.

As soon as he landed, Amy realized that the something was a butterfly made of silver. It must be Flora's brooch. And that wasn't all – clutched safely in the parrot's claws was Mum's ring.

Amy was delighted. "You're fantastic," she said, as she took the stolen goods from him. "I'm sure Inspector Lake would be proud of you." Then she headed for the sheep's field.

"Now we've got the evidence, we'd better talk to the thief."

The clan spread out as if they were just talking to the sheep. Then they gradually closed in on the magpie. The bird didn't realize what was happening until it was too late. She looked around at Amy, Hilton and the cats. Then she flapped her wings and tried to fly away. But Plato was too quick for her. He circled over her head to stop her taking off.

"What's going on?" asked the bird. Her voice shook with fear and she was breathing fast. She was much less calm than the weasel had been.

"You've been stealing," said Amy, with what she hoped was a very stern expression.

The magpie stepped back in shock and folded her wings. "No, I haven't. I'm not a thief."

"So how do you explain these?" said Amy. She held the ring and the brooch out on the palm of her hand. "We found them in your nest."

"Quite legally," added Plato. "I had a search warrant."

But the magpie wasn't listening to him. Her beady eyes were fixed on the objects in Amy's hand. "My shinies," she murmured, as she walked towards them. "Pretty, pretty shinies."

Amy quickly put the ring and brooch in her pocket before the magpie could take them again. "They're not yours. You stole them."

"No, I didn't. I found them. They'd just been left lying around — nobody wanted them."

"Yes, they did," said Hilton. "And they were very upset when they found they were gone."

Willow stared disapprovingly at the black and white bird. "You can't take things just because you like them. It's not allowed."

"Oh," said the magpie, hanging her head in shame. "No one's ever complained before."

"Perhaps no one's ever caught you before," said Amy. "You've got to give everything back."

"Everything?" asked the magpie in a very small voice.

Plato gave a small cough. "I'm sure that's not necessary."

"Of course it is," said Isambard.

"No, it's not," said Plato. "All that's left in her nest are metal bottle tops, shiny sweet wrappers and silvery screws. It really is rubbish that nobody wants."

"But very pretty rubbish," said the magpie. "I like pretty things."

"So do I," said Amy. "Just like my mum likes that ring and Flora likes her brooch."

"I'm sorry," said the magpie. "I'll try not to take anything important in future." She paused for a moment with her head tipped thoughtfully to one side. Then she added, "But I'm not sure how to do that."

"Stay away from human houses," advised Willow. "Humans are careless. They leave things lying around that they want."

"That's right," said Bun. "My

human left a sardine lying around
on a plate and he was really cross when
I ate it."

The magpie nodded hard. "I'll do
that. I promise." She looked round at
the clan and added, "Is there anything
else I can do to make up for what I've
done wrong?"

Amy was about to say "no" when
she remembered the weasel. They still
hadn't taught *him* that stealing was
wrong. Perhaps the magpie could help
them do that. "Could you carry a
chicken's egg?" she asked.

"Of course she couldn't," said
Isambard. "Her beak's too small."

"No, it's not," said the magpie.
"It opens really wide." She gaped her

mouth as wide as she could to show him. "That's impressive," said Isambard. "You should be able to hold an egg easily." Then he looked thoughtfully at Amy and asked, "What are you planning?"

"To teach that weasel a lesson," she replied, as she led the way back to the henhouse. "But I've got to talk to the chickens first. The plan won't work unless one of them helps."

CHAPTER EIGHT

The clan found the chickens busily pecking up the food Amy had sprinkled on the ground earlier. Faith and Hope looked up to see what they wanted. Charity didn't. She just went on eating.

"We want to teach the weasel a lesson," Amy said. "So I need one of you to lay an egg."

Faith shook her head. "I laid one first

thing this morning. I don't think I can manage another."

Hope looked slightly cross. "I'm not sure that I would if I could," she said, with a toss of her head. "You broke the last one."

"I'm sorry," said Amy.

"It was an accident," said Hilton.

"And it was delicious," said Bun.

For a moment, Amy thought her plan was going to fail before it had even started. Then Charity gulped down the last grain of food and looked up. "I've probably got an egg in me," she said.

Amy was delighted. "We're going to do the same as last time," she explained. "But we'll stay well back until the last minute. The weasel will be more cautious this time, and we don't want him to guess it's another trap."

So the clan settled down well away from the henhouse, while Plato and the magpie flew high above, watching the ground for signs of the thief. When they were all ready, Charity went into action.

Luckily, she was an even better actor than Hope. She strutted into the henhouse and squawked loud and long while she was inside. Then she rushed out again, singing "Oh, what a beautiful egg!" at the top of her voice.

Amy held her breath, waiting. Would the weasel be too cautious to try to steal again today? Or would his taste for eggs make him ignore the risks?

Suddenly Plato flew upwards in a dramatic loop. It was the signal Amy had been waiting for. It told her the weasel was in the henhouse.

The clan moved in and surrounded the hole where he would come out. This time Bun lay down with his front legs close together. He wasn't going to let the thief escape under him again.

There was a scrabbling noise inside the henhouse. A second later, an egg tumbled out of the hole. It was closely

followed by the weasel. He put his
front feet on the egg, ready to roll it
away. Then he noticed the clan
blocking his escape route and
immediately tried to run back into
the henhouse.

But Faith was there before him. She
poked her head out through the hole so

quickly that he ran straight into her sharp beak.

"Ouch!" cried the weasel, as he rubbed his nose. "I'm getting really tired of you lot. You're making thieving very difficult."

"So why don't you stop?" said Amy. "We told you it's wrong to steal."

"It makes people unhappy," said Hilton.

"Especially when it's food," said Bun.

The weasel sighed as he leaned on the egg. "I've told you before. There's nothing wrong with stealing."

"Are you sure?" said Amy, waving her hand at the magpie flying high above them.

The bird spotted the signal and

swooped down from the sky. She grabbed the egg in her beak and pulled it out from under the weasel's front paws.

The weasel fell flat on his face. "Ouch!" he cried, rubbing his sore nose.

He watched angrily as the magpie flew off with the egg and landed on top of the henhouse. Then he shook his paw at her and shouted, "Come back, thief! You've stolen my egg."

"That's not a problem, is it?" said Willow, with a smile. "You just told us there's nothing wrong with stealing."

"That's when *I* was doing it. This is different. It feels wrong when someone steals from me."

Isambard stepped closer to the weasel and glared at him. "So how do you think it feels for others when you steal from them?"

The weasel backed away from the tabby cat until he bumped his bottom on Faith's beak. He gave a squeak of pain. Then he muttered in a very subdued voice, "It must feel really bad."

"Perhaps your dear old mum never got around to mentioning that," said Amy, gently.

"Perhaps she didn't," agreed the weasel. "But I think I will, when I'm a dad."

Plato pecked him gently on the ear. "What are you going to do now?"

The weasel looked at the  parrot, then at Amy and Hilton and the cats. "I'm going to move well away from you lot," he declared. "But don't worry – you've made your point. I'm also going to stop stealing eggs."

"I'm glad to hear it," said Amy, with a grin. She moved aside to let him escape and watched as he raced off into the distance.

"Your plan worked!" shouted the magpie. That wasn't a good idea. Opening her mouth to talk made her let go of the egg. It tumbled onto the roof of the henhouse and rolled down it.

"Not again," cried Hope, as it tumbled off the edge and plummeted downwards.

Amy jumped forward and caught the egg just before it hit the ground.

"No harm done," she said, as she held it up for everyone to see.

Nearly everyone sighed with relief. Only Bun looked disappointed. "I bet that would have tasted good," he said.

The chickens clucked their thanks as Amy popped the egg back in the henhouse. Then she waved goodbye to

the clan and ran back to the Primrose
to give Mum her ring.

Mum was thrilled when she saw it.
"Wherever did you find it?" she asked.

"Outside," said Amy, as vaguely as she could. She didn't want to go into details in case she was asked awkward questions.

Luckily, Mum seemed happy with that explanation. And so was Flora when she got back from the wedding the next day. The old lady was delighted to have her brooch back and delighted to see how well Amy had looked after her animals. But what pleased her most were the four golden brown eggs nestled in the straw in the henhouse – Faith, Hope and Charity had laid three more to join the one the

clan had rescued from the weasel.

Flora beamed at Amy. "You've worked wonders," she said. "You've got my girls laying again."

Amy smiled, and said nothing at all. The mystery of the disappearing eggs had to stay secret, just like the magic of her very special necklace.

Amy Wild, Animal Talker

Collect all of Amy's fun and fur-filled adventures!

The Secret Necklace

Amy is thrilled to discover she can talk to animals!
But making friends is harder than she thought...

ISBN 9781409504290

The Musical Mouse

There's a singing mouse at Amy's school! Can Amy
find it a new home before the headmaster catches it?

ISBN 9781409504306

The Mystery Cat

Amy has to track down the owners of a playful
ginger cat who's lost his home...and his memory.

ISBN 9781409504313

Coming soon

The Great Sheep Race

Amy's thought of a fab fundraiser for her school
fair – a Great Sheep Race! But will Amy whip the
sheep into shape before the big day?

ISBN 9781409504337

The Star-Struck Parrot

Amy is thrilled when she gets to be an extra
in a film being shot on the Island. But Plato
the parrot dreams of stardom too. Can Amy help
him land his perfect part?

ISBN 9781409504344

For more fun and furry
animal stories, log on to
www.fiction.usborne.com